The New Earth
And The 144000

By

Clinton Withrow JR.

Table of Contents

Foreword

"Truth is stranger than fiction, but it is because Fiction is obliged to stick to possibilities; Truth isn't."

Mark Twain

Since Earth's humble beginnings there has been a struggle going on here. As is such the case of any life that's seeded by a more advanced race of beings. At first all the other races and species were welcome on earth. Little did humans know, there was an enemy collecting intelligence about them and the earth's construct. The experiment was simple, will humans be drawn to the light or the dark? A struggle between two species, Sister races created about the same time, humans who are empathic baby gods in training verses reptilians who are vibrational masters. The earth was created for humans. The reptilians are colonizers or miners. As such, they wiggle into places they are not welcome. They manipulate to take over by converting one human at a time. Through war and death, they keep humans constantly fighting with each other. This lowers the collective consciousness of the whole planet. For the earth to rid herself of this infestation we must shed the old to build the new. This new earth is not a vibrational match for the reptilians. They will not be able to evolve or manifest into this higher vibrating reality. Many souls will be recycled during process. For the higher good of all the beings here, sacrifices will be made.

Which earth will be your future? The choice is yours to create. What do you want to manifest? What you think about expands.

My Awakening

As I started this journey into the awakening process at times, I thought I was going crazy. It's like trying to take a drink from a fire hose. Trying to comprehend the massive information that was coming in. It became very apparent after just a short while on this journey that there is a great deal of misinformation out there. This is not by accident; it is by design that this is our "reality". I saw that it was going to be paramount to be able to decipher fact from fiction as we strive to free humans from their enslavement.

The first order of business is to mediate and ask to be given the ability to discern the truth from the lies. There is a huge need to get the real information out here. Spirit has the ability to guide people to this knowledge as needed. Each one will find their truth in their own way and in their own time frame.

I speak of my graduation a lot and how I know what graduation is like to experience. This is the story of my journey to now. One night while in meditation a bright light came down from heaven. This light came with such speed that before I could take my next breath, it was before me. The light was all loving and all-knowing. It spoke to me telepathically yet it was as clear as any human ever spoke to me. I could hear the light. We talked about what and who I was. We talked about what this light being was and what I was to do. I was asked to tell this story. To be the one that speaks out against the systems. Volunteer to be the target. Thousands of people's beliefs will be challenged. Why would anyone agree to this? That's when this being showed me the love and light of the Creator. It's all the love you want but you will never get while you are earth bound, in the 3rd dimension.

If I had my choice, I would have never left the presence of the light that night. I would have stayed forever. And in that instant, I remembered where I came from and what was waiting when I transitioned. The story of Moses on the mount talking to a burning bush is this same story. There is a messenger that brings the story for the age. Each age is 2160 years. Most of all, I remembered what an honor it would be to be chosen for this mission. I was shown how hard it would be and that there would be things about my present life that I would be giving up, permanently. I was told that if I took this mission I would be divinely connected and protected at all times. The things I am to share are the abilities the human has to self-heal. Humans can heal their own bodies. Also, to show humans they have the ability to speak directly to the Divine. I am to speak about the indoctrination systems and the control systems that have so many beings enslaved in the 3rd dimensional paradigm. A prison made of their own thoughts.

I was told that great fame (which I don't want) and I would have to take the stage on the world scene. What we are doing here right now will be talked about for the rest of earths existence. All future generations will talk about what we did… There will be a new time marker added that signifies the beginning of the new earth. Great travel will be necessary. I do love to travel. I was told that everything in my life would be torn apart. Then my life could be rebuilt on a more solid foundation that will bring true happiness, an abundance of consciousness and much love.

There are many levels of enlightenment here in earth school. The level I have achieved in this lifetime is graduation from earthly boundaries. I now have the option of returning to Source, going to create new worlds or return to earth to help others on their paths. I was creating worlds before I came to earth, so I think I have graduated earth at least once before. We have worked so hard and long to get here, to ascend the human race to a level it has never been before. I want to enjoy a 5th dimensional lifetime on the new earth, or the Garden of Eden as it is told in the Bible. Which is slightly higher than the 5th dimensional energies about what we think of the 7th dimensional energies. These levels that don't really exist are compartmentalized by the linear thinking human.

It was with a heavy heart that I accepted this mission. My wish and prayer is that I will do a good job getting this information out. History will be the judge here.

For this opportunity, I have to give gratitude to the Creator, the Elohim or angel that came to me, to my team, my higher self, my guides and guardians. To all the beings of light that are here helping our ascension I am great full.

Love, life and light.

Introduction

Let me start by saying that this message and mission are straight from Source. The theme of my work is information and regaining lost knowledge to help guide humanity through this transformation into a higher vibrating reality. I receive messages from Source in varies ways such as meditation, quantum healing sessions with my clients, sessions of mine and while sleeping. I want to help explain and show proof that humans can heal themselves. We control our own destiny.

I am a Quantum Healing Hypnosis Technique practitioner, QHHT was developed by Dolores Cannon. I am the creator of the Cosmic Quantum Awakening technique of Quantum Healing. This is how I come to access all this high information. I am an Alchemist, an Astrologer and a Hermetic magician. To understand where humanity is to go, we must look at where we came from.

This book is the first step to understanding where humanity is presently at now and why. Ultimately where we are going? This is the story of Clinton Withrow Jr., and my graduation from earthly boundaries to my role in the ascension of humanity.

One Light, One Love.

Chapter 1

The Emerald Tablets of Thoth

Excerpted from the Emerald Tablets:

I speak of ancient Atlantis.

I speak of the days of the kingdom of shadows.

I speak of the coming of the children of shadows.

Out of the great deep they were called by the wisdom of the

Earth man.

Called for the purpose of gaining great power.

For in the past before Atlantis existed, men there

were who delved into darkness using dark magic.

Calling up beings from the great deep below us.

Forth came they into this cycle.

Unforeseen were they from another vibration.

Existing unforeseen by the children of Earth men.

Only through blood could they have formed being.

Only through man could they live in this world.

In ages past they were conquered by masters.

Driven below to the place whence they came.

But there were some who remained.

Hidden in spaces and planes unknown to man.

Lived they in Atlantis as shadows.

1

But at times they appeared among man.

Aye when the blood was offered,

They came to dwell among man in the form of man.

In the form of man, they amongst us.

But only to sight were they as to man.

Serpent headed... when the glamour was lifted.

But appearing to man as men among men.

Crept they into the councils,

Taking forms that were like unto men.

Slaying by their arts the chiefs of the kingdoms.

Taking their form and ruling over man.

Only by magic could they be seen.

Sought they from the kingdom of shadows to destroy man and rule in his place.

But know ye, the masters were mighty in magic.

Able to lift the veil from the face of the serpent.

Able to send him back to his place.

Came they to man to teach him the secret.

The WORD that only a man can pronounce.

Swift, they lifted the veil from the serpent.

And cast him forth from the place amongst men,

Yet beware the serpent liveth in a place that is open at times to the world.

Unseen they walk among thee in places where the rites have been said.

Again, as time passes onward shall they take the semblance of men.

Only the white master can control and bind them while in the flesh.

2

Thoth was an Egyptian priest king who survived Atlantis. Atlantis sinking was due to the fact that reptilians tried to drill underneath the firmament. This is not the "natural" cyclic changes like the one coming up. Research Mud Flood on YouTube. These buried buildings are all around the earth. This mud builds up or more accurately, the sinking of the buildings is from a massive vibrational change. This created what modern science terms liquefaction today. There are times during the grand solar minimum that the earth has the ability to change in an instant. Mountains rise out of the ocean, coastal lands flood and more. Complete change in our present geography in a matter of minutes, maybe hours. The last one was somewhere between 1750 to 1850. The only "people" with this knowledge are part of secret societies. The civil war as its told to us was a great big cover up of the last reset. The Freemasons have a record of this. While researching the topic, I saw many pictures from around the world showing them marching the streets after the reset, in all their regalia.

This is a journey I am on, compelled by Spirit and being guided by the Most High. I am a seeker of lost knowledge, a seeker of the truth. To understand where humanity is to go in the future, we must understand our past. Humanity in its present form is approximately 200,000 years old. There have been many forms of humans. Humanity was seeded from that which we call aliens. But in reality, more like our fathers and mothers, the Pleiadians seeded us in our original form. That life was experienced for approximately 50,000 years. This first incarnation of man was called Lemuria. At this time our bodies were less dense and more of a light body. Then humans started at about 50 percent DNA activation. Today we are just moving up from the 30 percent we were at during the dark ages to an average of about 45 percent. Some could be more and some can be less. We were taller as well. This was due to the fact that there was more oxygen here and much more positive energy. The collective has been lowered by design to try to limit our abilities. The many years of mining has destroyed earth's eco system. The oxygen content in the air now is lower. We are breathing less oxygen today than our ancestors. The colonizers are purposefully contaminating the air and water... Air and water quality are the main determination for the human's lifespan. This is why we had stories of giants, even as late as the 1900s. I have seen pictures of men twice as tall as they are presently. They were killed off to hide the truth from future generations. We were plunged into the age of darkness. This was done by the colonizers to enslave the human race.

Chapter 2

The Watchers

Now let us speak of the watchers or the aliens that watch over us. The watchers watch over the human race just as a parent watches over their child. Every race of beings was seeded by other aliens in the universe. Everything has lineage back to Source. As we humans will one day in the future seed life somewhere else in the galaxy.

In the book of Enoch, it says that the watchers are angels dispatched to watch over the humans on earth. Let us reframe this. Some of the aliens that were dispatched and responsible for watching over us decided to join the incarnation process here on earth. Taking the human avatar, they were as gods among the newly developing earth human. The earth human who could be likened to having the consciousness of a teenager was joined by a fully developed consciousness. The earth human had no choice but to be the slave to the much smarter, fallen angels. After this happened, the controlling councils that be decided to wipe the earth plane and reset to start over. No one would actually die since we are eternal and reincarnate over and over again. This is the Noah story from the epic of Gilgamesh from Sumeria. There have been many floods from the resets that come every 400 years. The "flood" that came after this reset was not successful in wiping out the Nephilim or the fallen ones. It was these fallen ones that decided to call up from the great deep, the reptilian beings from a different incarnation.

This is why great civilizations magically sprang up out of nowhere, without any developmental history. These fallen

5

angels or aliens are what the world would refer to as dark workers and the angels that did not intrude are called lightworkers. Both light and dark know there is but one true Creator God in the multiverse. Today we mostly call God, Source or Creator or the All which sounds unusually like Allah. In Egypt she was called Ra. Yes, I said she. Now in our history books we are told that Ra was a man, As well as the Christian god as being a man. This is not the case. The darkness switches everything 180 degrees from truth. They use polarity to polarize the people for control purposes.

Let's take a look at a few examples. The part of the earth we live in is not a ball flying through space, it is flat and we are inside. This is where the inner earth and Agartha stories come from. We are inner earth. This is also how the big fish tank could be so easily flooded. Earth is a god school. Imagine if you had a bunch of baby gods running around trying to figure out how to use their god powers? This is why we are surrounded by water. The sky is blue because on the other side of the firmament is water, lots of water. We are able to be flooded at a moment's notice, if we get out of control. You would definitely want a fail safe in case the baby gods get out of control. This is also why it is so dense here. This is for our protection from ourselves. As we ascend and move into what people are calling new earth, this density will be lessened for those that are evolving. The ones among us ascending will experience a higher vibrating reality. Those that won't be ascending are the fifth graders staying in the 3rd dimension. Another point is that NASA trains in water, because water is space. As we are surrounded by water, we do not leave here in the physical, although some seem to think they can. At some point the Nazi led Reptilians might even try to flood the earth again. This is also why the powers that be are always showing you alien invasion movies. There will be more ships that come down to the earth plane. The powers that be would like you to be in fear of this and start a war with them.

Let's examine the movie Avatar. The human mind goes into the alien avatar. In reality it's the alien mind that goes into the human avatar. It's funny how the aliens shown are of the blue Pleiadian type, just like so many in my quantum sessions have described. How about Orpah's production company Harpo, Oprah spelled backwards. Do you think she's part of the elite? Or, love spelled backwards is evol or evil. They told us milk was good for us, but in reality, it is difficult for many humans to digest. Eat meat, it's the best source of protein. No, no its not and in general, it's very unhealthy. The WHO, the World Health Organization listed red meat as a class one carcinogen. And what about global warming? It's actually getting colder as we head into a mini ice age. These ice ages are imperative for the fish tank in which we live. Frigid temperatures are necessary to revitalize the water. Anyone that has a salt water fish tank knows that when you don't do a water change life starts to die. Anyone seen the news from around the planet about the fish and marine life dying off like crazy? It's time to change the water. This is a love story. If this cycle didn't happen there would be no life in the future. And the powers that be have known about this reset and covered up cycle. They have done this time and time again. They use it as population culling. They keep control over the number of their indebted slaves. I could write an entire book just on how things we are taught in our government indoctrination camps or schools are 180 degrees backwards. When this truth is brought forward and told to men their first reaction is one of anger. It goes against the ingrained belief system that is installed in the first eight years of a child's life. This reaction is called cognitive dissonance and is a side effect of the brainwashing.

The Creator is both a male and female polarity as we all are, on the other side of the veil. This is symbolized by the androgyny in Hermetics. As above, so below. It takes a woman's body to incubate a human on earth. Yes, a man is needed for the "creation". This shows us that the Creator is a female aspect. Everything here mirrors the upper dimensions. It takes a woman nine months to grow the baby. Nine symbolizes beginnings and endings. This is why all prices have nines at the end. This is the magic used against the unsuspecting public so businesses can keep more of your hard-earned money.

Let us pause and discuss time. The past, present and future all occur at the same moment. The notion of time doesn't really exist but, time lines do exist. The past, present and future do exist, at once. If you want to find the secrets to the universe think in the terms of energy frequency and vibration. Nikola Tesla said, "The day science begins to study non-physical phenomena, it will make more progress in one decade than in all the previous centuries of its existence."

That day is upon us!

Chapter 3

The Story of Me

To tell this story, I must speak of how I came to be in the present. I was born into this incarnation to an American Indian mother and a Caucasian father. My mother died when I was about a year and a half old. I say about, because I really don't know much about my mother or her family. The first time I saw a picture of my mother, I was only twelve years old, it was on her grave stone. Our family lived in Beckley, West Virginia. My childhood was a lot like a roller coaster being that my father raised me as a single parent. All the while he was seeking love and his own life path. My father is the most mechanically proficient people I ever meet, no doubt in some of his incarnations he has surely created great technology. I was raised a Southern Baptist. My indoctrinated belief structure started when I was very young. I was taught that I lived in sin and I needed to repent to be saved. The God I was taught about was angry man god and lived in the sky. He wanted to destroy the earth. I was taught that a killer or a rapist can just ask for forgiveness and all the karma from these actions are magically wiped out. This is so damaging to any human as this is never the case and it leads many souls down a dark path. This is far from what I know as the truth today. The philosophy that you can kill or harm someone and just ask for forgiveness to be free from consequence is trapping souls in a karmic hamster wheel. When the soul transitions after death that soul has to answer for whatever it did. Period. Karma has to be paid.

I made the decision to run away from home at age fifteen because of the extreme physical and emotional abuse. My father was a military veteran that was very scarred from war and the loss of my mother and many years of hardcore drug use. After getting a beating from my dad one day I was taken from school and placed into custody of the state. Speaking of war, it is used to dumb down the masses. It is also a tool to depopulate and generate money. Poverty is also used to keep the population ignorant. The trauma from war makes the consciousness drop down. I lived in a state-run group home. When I turned eighteen, I joined the United States Army for lack of other options. I wonder if it I designed this life this way on purpose... My need to feed the desire to see and experience the world was realized.

Chapter 4

The Principle of Cause and Effect

Every cause has its effect and every effect has its cause. Everything happens according to law. Chance is but a name given for a law not recognized. There are many planes of causation but nothing escapes law. This is what people call karma and dharma. There is no such thing as a coincidence. Every single thing happens for a very specific purpose.

After joining the US Army. I was stationed at Fort Campbell in Kentucky. First at the 187th airborne infantry as a combat medic. After about three years I felt the urge to seek more experiences. One day I saw group of men doing PT or physical training. They were running by my billets, in a small group. They had a very different uniform. I decided to follow them. They led me to a group of buildings that were very unremarkable in appearance. I went up to one of the doors and knocked. A very tall young man opened the door. He had no name tag on and extremely long hair. I asked him what their unit was and what they did? To which the young man didn't answer, only looked at me funny and started laughing. Feeling extremely awkward, I explained to him that I was in the Infantry right down the street and that I was currently a medic. I added that I was looking to do something else with my military career. I knew I wanted something more meaningful. At which time the young man said that they were a special operations aviation unit, the 160th SOAR. I, by chance, had knocked on the medical platoon's door. This unit works directly with tier one assets. The assets are also known as operators inside the community like the Navy SEALs, Delta Force, Air force Pararescue, Combat Controllers, Marine Force Recon, Virginia Militia are all soldiers that are put into harm's way. They are lured by the black gear, the Velcro and the willingness to test one's self in the crucible of battle. I was told there were no openings and the doors were shut in my face. Me, being the person that I am, didn't take no for an answer. I knocked on that door twice a week, every week, for an entire year. Eventually they gave me the opportunity to try out. After trying out and being accepted, I started learning advanced life-saving techniques. I traveled around the world. I will not speak any more about the unit and what they do. They are a secret for a reason, but I will say it was an honor to serve with the other volunteers.

Chapter 5

The Awakening

With new eyes we look at the world like a blind man that sees for the first time. Sometime around 2012, I started seeing and experiencing some crazy phenomena. I was working the night shift as a trouble man for the largest power company in the US. I would look at the moon and notice it would look different to me. The moon I saw had halos around it and called to me to stare back. One day I woke up, walked outside, looked at the world and it was literally with fresh eyes, new eyes. What I saw was not what I served in the armed services to protect. There were lies everywhere. There was death at every doctor's office. Lies in the news. I started having allergic reactions to processed foods. So many cancer-causing chemicals have been added to our food sources plus most food has been genetically modified. There is a secret war on humans especially in the United States. America will be ground zero in this spiritual war.

Driven by some unknown force, I started searching and I found many truthier sites. They tell some fact but polarize the human so they can be controlled. No doubt that is their purpose. Recently Alex Jones just got taken off the internet. Good riddance! That guy did nothing but add a little truth to spread major fear and lies. So, after realizing these traps were everywhere, I asked my Higher Self to give me the ABILITY to discern truth from lies. Now, I've got to pause to say be careful what you ask for. My discernment got so strong that in passing I would see something on television and I'd speak out and say that's a lie! This would happen before I could catch myself. Often it was not the most opportune moment. It wasn't ideal since I worked with a bunch of corn-fed country boys that didn't take well to the whole enlightenment concept. Three quarters of the people working there were Freemasons. You can research the blue lodges, which control all of the lower level operations within the organization.

My hunger for truth and knowledge was insatiable. I would read for hours and search the internet even longer. The Hermetic principal of polarity is what the elite use to steer the masses. Almost every human is polarized against something and for something else. Ever notice how every FREE society in our present world has two parties? It must be a coincidence. It's the illusion of choice. Remember, I said there are no coincidences. None.

I spent over twenty years building, repairing and maintaining power lines. I learned a lot about our power system. Here is what I learned, the AC power system is a quantum power source that's feed by a dirty, polluting 3rd dimensional generator. Let's look at the Tesla Coil. We feed it with 120 volts and it creates sparks and lightening like effects. Could we use the 180-degree backwards principle here? Let us see a transformer as a mirror. As a lineman, when I had to change out a bad transformer, we would disconnect the 7kv or high voltage side. Then we had to isolate or disconnect the secondary side, or the 120/240-volt side. Because, if we did not do this the transformer would be back-fed by a 120-volt source that would produce 7 kv on the high voltage side. What goes in one side is mirrored on the other side. The voltage depends on the number of coils in the transformer. Let's apply this to the Tesla coil. What if we feed it with lightening style electricity? Would it produce the 120 volts that we feed it with currently? I hypothesize that the answer is yes. The answer to free power has been hidden right in front of our eyes this whole time. The answer was here for us to discover when the time was right. Now is that time, now.

14

The answer here is atmospheric electricity. We put up a pole and that electricity is fed into a Tesla coil backwards; from the present way we are using it today. I uncovered this truth while researching Tartaria. I came across paintings that showed they had atmospheric power as late as the 1700's. No doubt the darkness used this periodic cool period to re-frame civilization into a lower vibrational existence. When the human is traumatized physically or emotionally it puts the human consciousness into a much lower vibration. As we are all co-creating our reality, this is what the darkness uses. That is why we are where we are today.

A power transformer set up the way shown, could power one to several homes. Non-grid free power is in our grasp at this time on the planet now. We can use thermal power for generation. Drill two kilometers down, install a circulation system and fill geo-thermal pipe with liquids that nearly boil at room temperature. We currently have this in place, free power that's good for the environment and self-sustainable. Free energy. Freedom from slavery. Free from having to go to a work place for 40 plus hours a week to pay the utility company and other bills, just to exist. The Creator did not design it this way. But in the future God's plan will be restored here on earth.

Chapter 6

God are You listening?

I'd like to speak about the earth plane now. Earth is a graduate school where we go to learn how to use our creative powers and learn about the god within us. From the moment we are separated from Source we are on a journey to return to Source. We also come to earth to learn love, compassion and to help each other. Nowhere else in the multiverse can you learn as fast as you do on earth. Earth is a grand experiment started long ago. The Creator endowed earth with free will. Free will does not exist anywhere else in the universe like it does here. We are presently the youngest race of beings in the multiverse. As we talk about humans, we must first look up the word human. Hu is Arabic for God and man means hand. So human means God hand. What that should tell you is no one is coming save you. It's YOUR job to save yourself first then the earth next. "Knowledge is to know the ledge that bridges the gap between the hidden in the seen", author unknown.

Hue also means color or shade. We are told that humans are created in God's image. The profane, unenlightened or my favorites the No-Mag, take these words literally. They think God is in the shape of a human form. This is not what was to be conveyed. This is not the truth. The way it is supposed to be interpreted is that God, Source or the All is light and is inside every human being. A spark or a sliver of that same divine light created everything in the multiverse. We were created in God's image. God is a creator therefore man is a creator. For those of us that have felt the privilege of standing in the presence of that light, we know that God is all love. It's everything we want and need at the soul level. For me, when the light came down from heaven, I was standing in front of the Creator's light, an Elohim or an angel. I didn't want it to end. However, I knew I had a job to do and a mission to accomplish on earth, in my present incarnation. As I said goodbye an immense feeling of sorrow overcame me. Then I was shown the truth. I now knew what was waiting for me when I was done. This knowing gave me purpose. This knowing is what drives me, gives me the courage to stand up and speak out against all the lies that we are presently indoctrinated with. The stories told in the Bible like Moses on the mountain talking to a burning bush may not be accurate. The burning bush is a representation of the light from an angel that came to bring a message to Moses.

Speaking of Moses, I encourage all to go on YouTube and search TransformOtion channel about the video on QHHT. A medicine woman in exodus gets a message from God. That message tells the true story of the Moses that killed his step- mother. Then Moses was taken in to keep him from being orphaned. That's a little different than the version in the King James Bible. You will see a story of killing, drugs, sex and blood magic. I feel that the story of Moses on the mountain talking to the burning bush was really someone else, completely different than Moses. All the information we have is so convoluted. This Moses is not the same Moses on the mount, they are two different people from very distant times.

The Cross of Christianity is a representation of this light. It is so bright that when you look at it, it's light appears as a cross. The presently used symbol of the cross with the bottom longer is not what the Maltese cross looked like. The Christian cross of today is telling you that they polarized it to the earth. That is why the cross is longer on the bottom. If you compare the Christian cross to an Ankh where the top is a circle. A circle tells us two things; a circle is the representation of the Creator and that we reincarnate. The straight line at the top of the Christian cross tells us they are hiding reincarnation from their people.

I would like to talk about the human to God connection. Many today think this is a belief structure. I contend it only a belief structure until you actually seek God. To seek God, you must go within. This is the reason the side of your head near your eye is called the temple. We enter a temple for worship. After seeking and making this connection, there is a knowing. I have no doubt, in any part of my being, who the one true Creator God is. God does not ask for or need worship or praise and she definitively doesn't need money. We glorify and give praise because the love felt is so strong. The love we feel is powerful. God is only love. If you are with love you are with God. If your actions are out of love then you are acting as God wishes.

When I started practicing magic, I never thought it would lead to finding God. I thought I was going to conjure up entities and demons then command them for materiel gain. Yes, I said it, I started this so I could benefit. Little did I know; it does not work that way. The hermetic way is self-transformation. By going within and making changes it literally changes the reality you experience.

There was a time when I was approached by a very powerful and dark entity promising all the riches that could be had. My answer was no, I did not sign any soul contracts for materiel gain. I chose the high road. We as godlike humans have the ability to control our future and our path. I do all of these things and I accept my mission. The mission that I signed a soul contract to come here and complete.

It's something that has been under the surface of my being the whole time. Waiting for the time of the awakening, the time of LIGHT. Behold it is upon us. WOW, what a beautiful time to be on this planet! The light will be victorious. Guided by the Most High. It is already done. The dark are the only ones that don't know this yet. Speaking of the darkness, when the grand experiment of duality or light and dark was started, it was in order to fast track the evolution of humans. Over time the darkness grew to epic proportions, becoming way out of balance for actual learning. Earth became a prison planet full of brainwashed slaves caught in a karmic mind trap.

Controlled by fear, people are on a karmic cycle that they cannot break. Fear of death, fear of imprisonment, fear is used for everything. Let's speak esoterically from a magical standpoint. The darkness must use fear as their magic, since they are not gods and never will be. A god has the ability to create realty through thoughts and emotions. Empathy is what we use if we want to control or create a situation, like when the propaganda machines and the dark workers start spreading fear all over the planet. They capture fear energy and use that negative energy in dark magic ways against those who emitted the fear. In effect their fear energy caused what they were afraid of to be manifested into reality. By each and every one of us conquering fear, we take their power away. Speaking of the darkness, they claim they have created the major megaliths but in reality, the light is the creative Source everywhere. Anything that is grand and beautiful was created by the light. The only thing the darkness ever created was slavery, death, pain and lies. But the darkness is good at claiming they made things that the light actually created. Because the light created us, this on some level is a true statement. The light by nature are closer to our creative powers. This means that all humans are natural creators as we were made in the image of the Creator.

Chapter 7

Quantum Healing

I started my journey into Quantum healing for the access to higher knowledge. I really didn't understand the healing abilities that were hidden inside the quantum realm. I wanted to explore the unknown. The first time I saw a session, I immediately recognized that these practitioners were going into the magical realm. The Theta realm is a deep state of hypnosis. The reason I recognized this is because I am a Hermetic magician, and most of all I am a WARRIOR of the Light.

Through the dark ages, the light had to hide our knowledge and our magic. There would come a time when it was going to be needed. Necessary for the biggest, grandest, spiritual battle of all time. In times past as the balance would swing from the darkness to light, the controllers would just polarize the societies from matriarch to patriarch. This control and manipulation would keep going. This is clearly evident when we look into the past. Men would wear white powder wigs trying to appear as women. This was because society was polarized to keep earth from gaining a natural balance between the male and female. Any polarized society or person can easily be manipulated.

We are in the time of the ascension when freedom is coming to this planet. A time of no more darkness. The darkness will never be in control again. The crazy thing is the brainwashed humans here seem to love their enslavement. Most would not want their life to change. They are comfortable with their monotonous existence. Humans think they have security with their bank accounts and their government to protect them from the perceived bad guys. The bad guys, that the dark created. The absolute truth is there is no guarantee of security. These humans are getting ready to experience this first hand. Graduation is upon them. Time to pick light or dark. Choose good or evil. To kill others and take, or to come together to create, love and help each other.

As I started into the Quantum healing realm, I was drawn to the Dolores Cannons modality Quantum Healing Hypnosis Technique or QHHT. I started seeing clients and within the first ten clients, I had a client become very disturbed during a session. Her higher self, showed her something from her past life. At least I thought it was her higher self. I was able to calm her down and proceeded with the normal steps. You're taught to tell the client it's okay, you don't have to experience this again. You have already lived this life. You are just observing it now. A few weeks later the client was having a serious emotional issue. When we talked it was easy to figure out it was triggered by the session. In another client session I asked if I could speak to the client's higher self, her higher self said no. I thought that was weird. I thought all higher selves wanted this healing and the direct connection, none the less I moved on. The next anomaly I noticed was when I asked a higher self for a body scan. I was told that the client was healthy and didn't need one. I'm scratching my head at this point. Paying over a thousand dollars to take an online class and watch some videos, does not prepare practitioners for these situations. Note to self, I can create a better system. While researching information online my higher self, guided me to Alba Weinman. I watched some of her videos. She was asking to look for colors and then talking to them. I knew there was something else going on with these sessions. I was going to look at these energies and talk to them too. Now being a Hermetic magician, I knew there were spirits and energy all around us.

There is even a whole system of magic called necromancy that deals specifically with spirit conjure.

Freemasons also deal with spirit conjure. Just google the Ars Notoria or the 72 demons of the Goetia and start reading. These Free Masons are called free because they don't follow the same rules as the slaves. Mason because they are building the world for the archons. Most of the Free Masons are not reptilian but naive humans that use their free will to speak an oath to join. Then through the use of polarity during the initiation ceremony they take the Mason into a fear state. Once in that fear state it is easy for a dark entity to enter the vessel and start to assimilate that soul. Once this process starts that soul is forever lost to the dark energy. I have done many sessions on Freemasons and they cannot be healed from this condition. They are lost forever and will be recycled.

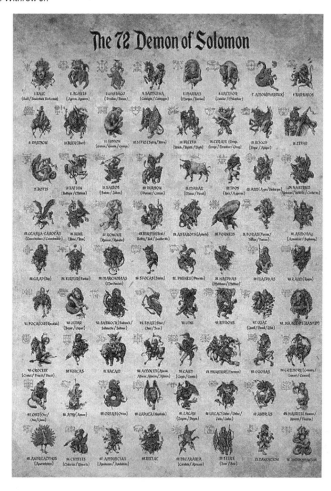

Speaking of necromancy, in ancient times after the fall of man or duality descended onto the planet, there was a split in the priest Magicians of Atlantis. On one side you had the Magi or the light and on the other side the Necromancers or the darkness. Before the fall of darkness, they were unified but after they went their separate ways. A quick search on a Masonic tracing board will show a checkerboard floor. This is to represent the battle between light and darkness. The Duke of Kent is the head of Freemasonry worldwide, or Prince Edward of the Royal Family. This is your incarnate physical

24

controllers of the planet. There are many secret levels as well. They are without a doubt Reptilians but it's important that we stress the fact that all races of the multiverse are made up the light and dark forces. The truth is in the name Queen Elizabeth. EL means god. Liza short for lizard. Beth in Hebrew is house. This translates to god lizard house. These beings have killed, lied, bribed and used spirits to do their bidding on this planet. These are the bad reptilians. They have a hive mindset. Like the BORG from Star Trek. I said "bad" because not all reptilians are bad. The reptilians do not have any empathy while mentally healthy humans do have empathy. Reptilians came from Mars, where they destroyed most of that planet. They will not be a vibrational match for the new earth energies. Hence the lower vibrational realities will be closed out at some point. This is why the elites are talking about going to Mars. Mars is where the reptilians came from. Every elite you hear talking about going to mars is reptilian. They print articles for humans to read which generates energy towards their dark goals. They plan on leaving planet before the reality split but before the destruction of the 3rd dimensional world when it will be closed out forever. They have done this 4 times before. Now they are trying to do the same here.

Anyone remember the TV series from the 80s and 90s called V? It was about reptilians that looked human. Lies in the media and truth in movies. So many references to reptilians hiding among men here on earth. We as magicians can unlock our ability to see them with our human eyes. The reptilians vibrate very high. So high they must eat meat to keep their vibration down. In the ancient past this was one of the ways be spotted. Today they have convinced humans to eat rotten flesh so they can hide in plain sight. To overcome this masking of themselves we must use the first law of Hermetics. Mentalism is the first law. Through our sheer will and asking for our human eyes to be able to see the reptilians, we can un- glamor them when in their presence. For me, their eyes start to change and their pupils get narrow like a snake's eyes look. Their eyebrows will raise up. They try to raise their vibration to counter our will, their energy starts to phase in and out. This is why they are called shape shifters. In reality it's just a glamour that comes from their ability to raise their vibration to an extremely high level. They gain this ability through the sacrifice of animals and young children. This is why there are so many missing. I must tell of the first time I knowingly meet one. In meditation I asked for the ability to see meet these beings. I also asked for the ability to understand who and what these things are. Careful what you ask for… Out of nowhere I get a call one day and it's this woman that is very beautiful and very small in stature. During the pre-talk she tells me that she's 56. I was like wow because she looked 25 to me. During the session, I try to do the QHHT method of past life regression and she doesn't see anything just blackness. After a little while of her visualizing nothing but blackness, I call in the higher self and during our conversation she tells me that she keeps her avatar at age 27. I was like that's awesome because I was researching how to stop and reverse the aging process. After the session she sits up and I am talking to her, I say I'm sorry I didn't get her better information or a past life. As I am talking her eyes start to look funny and change. The more I concentrated on it the more it was phasing in and out of my vibrational reality. I went to meditation immediately after and sought information. She was a good reptilian that came to steer me on my path and I gave her technology that would feed the new world. I could never reach her again after she left. I say thank you for all the different beings help. Not all reptilians are bad. The dark wants us to think they are all bad, but that is not the truth. There are good reptilians here with us now.

As I started talking to these entities, I noticed some very common things. Discarnate souls as I call them, all had names and most could tell you how they died and at what age. I also identified some other types as well. Thought forms as I call them, are energies that are created by the client. Now to understand this we must understand how energy works here on Earth. First of all, we are creators created in God's image. So, by proxy, we are creators as well. All energy release here is in a circuit. What we put out is what will come back. If we vibrate love out then love is what comes back to us. If we vibrate out hate then hate comes back to us. Now magicians know techniques that can stop energy from returning to them. That's another book to come later on magic and how to use our divine powers to create responsibly. If the client gets into a low vibrational state through physical trauma, emotional trauma or disease. The poisons are abundant everywhere that lower the vibration of a client and if the client feels a certain way, whether it be anger or hate from these emotions. The energy that vibrates out comes back to them eventually. Remember we said that all energy is a circuit. Each human creates their own reality that they experience.

When the energy returns to the client it attaches to their etheric or light body. At this point the client can face the emotions associated with it and raise their vibration to release the energy. Very few have this ability to self heal this way. If they feel self-pity and sorrow however, that will feed this negative energy and make it stronger. Now this is where it gets compounded. When clients go into a low vibrational state, they open themselves up to be a target for these entities to walk in and attach. The entities can see the energies present in the etheric body of the client. Once attached they use the thought form energies created by the client against them to manipulate the emotions of the client.

I have also identified another two types. I have saved these for last as they are less common. The first is a dark gray to mostly black energy. We'll call these demons for lack of a better word to describe them. They are super low vibrating and usually don't talk or share their name, but occasionally they do. I have found that if the practitioner asks who sent you and where did you come from it triggers their memory. The client will see the entities journey in reverse, from the necromancer that sent them. Occasionally I have caught them while traveling, this is when they hitch a ride on a low vibrational human to get to another location. In this aspect they usually talk. Like Molech the babylonian god of child sacrifice. Lets say light worker 1 molech returned to source. The last one that I want to talk about resembles the scarab's hieroglyphics from Egypt and I am very convinced these symbols were left to either warn or to brag about their accomplishments. The Scarab beetle entity was attached to the aura of a client that was a Freemason.

The entities which have names and that talk with colors that are lighter type. These are not always souls that didn't cross over. Some are soul fractals. Let me explain, this is when an avatar dies. The spirit, if it chooses and knows how to, will cross back to the place of waiting. Which most clients describe as the clouds. Then they go back to the light, also called the cave of creation. Here they are greeted by their relatives and receive healing. Then they do a life review. At which time they watch what they did to others. Next, they are made to feel what they made the other person or people felt. You will judge yourself. You will reap what u sowed. Not some angry man god in the sky. And this makes perfect sense because honestly who is harder on ourselves than us? Next, we are allowed a time to rest and reflect. Then we go on to plan our next life experiences with our soul groups directed by source. As the soul goes back to Source or the light it leaves everything negative here on the Earth plane this is what we call a soul fractile. This is to minimize the negative that goes back to Source. This is where the soul fractals come from. Now this is the way the Creator designed this realm to be. To exaggerate our emotions so we must learn to deal with them or fail. This is to teach us to teach ourselves. The problem here is the Freemason and Jesuit created religion of Christianity and Islam. Both of these religions used to be one and the darkness separated them to be used against each other to foment war at a later date. Hence the reason they are fighting and occupying the same land at the present time, This is by design.

After identifying all these different types of entities, I noticed that when I removed them, miraculous things started happening to clients. People started telling me they no longer had pain they had for most of their lives. Also, they no longer had to take medication to provide relief and stopped all on their own. Absolutely miraculous healing was occurring. Then it dawned on me this was the healings that Dolores Cannon was talking about. We now have the ability on the planet to heal with intent and unity through Spirit provided belief. The biblical stories of Jesus healing people have similar tales. It is said that Jesus and his disciples healed by casting out demons. Interesting isn't it that with Cosmic Quantum Awakening technique we are removing entities and thought forms from clients. Two important pieces must exist for the healing to happen. First, the client must believe they can heal and second, the client must ask for the help. If the client believes they can heal then are healed. It is that plain and simple. I figured out how to cure disease and illness by asking one simple question to the Higher Self, who created this illness? Who created this disease? The answer is always the same. The client did. At that moment they now understand they created it and therefore they can uncreate it. I can't tell you how many times I asked for a client to be healed in a certain body part or from a specific disease only to hear we cannot! Why I would ask, only to be answered with, they don't believe they can heal so we cannot heal them. I would ask do you think you could lessen the symptoms for them and to this they would say yes, we will do all that what we can.

Chapter 8

Nikki

I had a client named Nikki; she was in a terrible way, dealing with all kinds of crazy emotions. She was almost frantic when she arrived. So, after the pre talk she tells me that she had a lot of resistance about coming. Fear and anxiety had almost stopped her. We started the session and very shortly after coming off the cloud she freaks out, The cloud is the movement vehicle for the qhht induction. Nikki gets overly emotional. At first, I am thinking this is an imbalanced conscious mind trying to control the situation. But guided by my Higher Self, I stopped the past life regression and calmed her down and induced her into hypnosis again. Once she was deep and went straight to her Higher Self and asked for a body scan. I asked it to look for colors. There was color found, in fact a lot of color was revealed and asked to exit. I removed them all until I had her etheric body clear as possible. She still had some residue from a thought form. Her higher self, asked to leave a little so she could learn her lesson and deal with it in her conscious mind, then I ask her Higher Self why did you show her that life in Egypt? Nikki's Higher Self said it had not shown her that. The dark entities had manipulated and shown her that life, Not every thought or emotion is yours.. On top of that, they made her feel like she had hurt people. Finally, proof that there were some things going on unseen by other practitioners. It was in this moment that the Cosmic Quantum Awakening clearing and healing technique was created. I couldn't wait to get this information out. So many would be helped by this information. So, I started posting the results of my sessions on the one forum that quantum practitioners have. Wow, the response was crazy! No one believed me. The other practitioners started attacking me. I don't believe in entities, they would say. Why don't these show up in my sessions, they ask. I responded, have you looked for them? And the answer was always a resounding NO, so i would tell the other practitioners to look for them. Then I had a practitioner tell me that I shouldn't be messing with these dark entities. So, I meditated on this and asked for guidance. In my sessions, messages started coming through with answers. I was told it's like cleaning your room. If you never cleaned it, it would be very dirty. When I asked if we should be doing this on a regular basis I was asked, should you clean your room on a regular basis? I noticed every time I posted something on the quantum healing practitioners page or offered my opinion; the response was a barrage of enemy fire from all sides. Could there be an underlying issue as to why the forum moderators would attack my posts. Like they were intentionally not wanting this information to come out. I was even told that Dolores Cannon forbid her practioners from talking about entities, so clearly she was aware of this. Just like in combat, when we get close to the target things start to pick up and fire comes from all directions. After getting tired of this constant attacking, I started posting the sessions. Practitioners would be able to listen and judge for themselves. This did not go over well with the forum owner who uses the forum to push her own modality to increase her personal sales. It wasn't long after I got kicked off of her forum. They don't want us to talk about

flat Earth, fight club or entities **. . .**

Chapter 9

The Holy Trinity

After sharing this information new and interested practitioners started coming forward. They wanted to get clearing and healing sessions and from me. They also encouraged me to teach them the techniques that I had learned/discovered. On this journey I learned many different things. Not all human avatars have a connection to Source. Although I do believe with a lot of inner work, we all can have this connection to Source. Souls here are at many different levels of development. There are very few truly devolved fully functional human beings here. Spirit says less that 1 k. If a younger soul gets a session done, In that instant their higher self is created. The bridge to it is also created. To get this connection one must bring balance and stillness to the mind. Clint you might ask, how does one do this? First let's talk about the Divine masculine and the Divine feminine and Source or the holy Trinity. It was hidden right here before our eyes the whole time. We must balance these forces to have our connection to Source or God. We can speak directly to our Creator any time we desire. We can also communicate as well with our ancestors, angels and our spirit guides. The male polarity of the brain is the conscious mind. It's the part of the brain that's loud like a man and is responsible for the force to create movement for creation. The feminine polarity of the brain is the subconscious. It's the part of the brain that knows everything that's going on and is really running things just like a woman, this aspect of the consciousness is the part that creates reality and creates the dream of what the human wants to experience and how to go about creating it. While the male or conscious mind is talking the loudest, the subconscious is behind the scenes doing all the work. This is also hidden in the tarot cards. For example, on the lover's card, the man looks at the woman, she is looking up to God. It is through the woman that the man's connection to God spawned from the conscious mind. The true and real holy Trinity.

There was such a large number of practitioners that couldn't have successful sessions, I was amazed. These people were guiding others through realms they themselves had no experience in. It's like going to a mechanic to fix your car that has never driven a car. Not exactly an ideal choice. I would try to explain how these practitioners could do the work to bring balance, getting their own connection to Source. They would get upset and tell me that it just didn't resonate with them. Their belief in God was just fine, they didn't need to do anything more or different. Unfortunately, there are people guiding clients to this connection with their Higher Self and Source but have not bridged the gap themselves. I urge all clients to ask their practitioners if they have had a session and was it positive. If they cannot give you access to seeing a successful session of themselves, I would find another practitioner.

This is set up on purpose for all souls. We must seek the connection to our Higher Self once we become self-aware that we are eternal. If we seek it out, in time you will establish this connection to your High Self. Earth is like a kindergarten through College level school where we all look alike and go to the same school. This is earth school, for gods in training.

We are here to learn our own individual lessons and to learn them at our own pace. No one is going to come save you. What would they be getting saved from? Learning their own lessons; for their own good? It's their lessons to be learned. By convincing people some being will save you, this stops you from looking inward, trying to save yourself. The dark forces that were supposed to only bring a certain amount of darkness here got greedy. They became very power hungry and they took too much, they killed too much. This convoluted the entire system. After they set out on a global conquest killing and raping their way through the indigenous peoples wiping out the handed down knowledge. This is why you are reading this. Every light worker is behind enemy lines here. We are so powerful that when we wake up and band together, nothing will stop us!!! We are supported by all the forces of Light, angels, ascended masters and extra-terrestrials. The Garden of Eden will be restored, God's plan for heaven on Earth will be so. "So, mote it be".

Our Guidance system is our heart. Every human being has this built in. In our schools we are taught to not trust ourselves and we learn to ignore these heart feelings. This is the worst thing that can ever happen to any human. This is their ability to feel their way through this realm. This is the way their Higher Self guides them on their journey. Until we take back our children from the government run school system, we will not have control over our own future. People are doing this by the droves. Homeschooling is growing everywhere. The more the Elites push their Orwellian agenda the more it becomes to the people that they are slaves, subjects that others control. The more they lose control the more they will try to force their hand with the forced vaccinations and the unjust laws. This is exactly what will wake up the masses.

Chapter 10

Erma

I meet a fellow practitioner and instantly we vibrated at the very same frequency. It does not take much interaction for two light workers to resonate. After swapping sessions and learning from each other we decided to collaborate. The plan is to create a training program, teaching others that were yet to awaken about healing. Erma had figured out a lot of the same things that I had with the entities and thought forms. Her system was at a master's level and the average person could not learn that so we decided to use my simpler system. Erma is a true professional with the highest integrity and ethics. She is a Quantum Ninja! Every time I have a session, I learn something new. Specifically, about hypnosis and how The Cosmic Quantum Awakening movement, CQA is on the front lines of the battle between light and dark here in the earth school game as mentioned by Edgar Casey. The war of Armageddon. This war will be fought in the astral within the minds of men and women. This battle will take place in all planes of existence. The upper planes like the new Earth will be the spiritual battle, the 3rd dimensional level will have the actual physical battles, As above so Below. The truth is that the light has already won. Victory day for the light was June 1, 2018. They sent me a client for a session and they told me this information and also that we were under a new system of karma. That old karma was now turned off. Today we have super karma to assist the good and the dark. Those souls that still have lessons to learn such as not to lie, cheat, kill or steal etc. The dark energy will guide them to learn at a faster rate by giving them what they are thinking about, negative energy .

Their thoughts and their words will create their reality quickly. This causes the teaching to occur at an accelerated rate. The other side of the coin is that by SUPER karma being in place we can manifest whatever we are thinking about. If you do the inner work and meditate and have positive thoughts you will experience a positive reality. Now let discuss the Ascension. It comes every 400 years and is timed with the mini ice age also called the grand solar minimum. This is the time where souls in the Earth school can raise their vibrations through love and oneness. By controlling their thoughts, silencing their ego and conscious mind, they can elevate to the next vibrational frequency. This Ascension is a little different than all the ones in the past. We as a collective have been asked to evolve to a higher vibration. We are tired of all the slavery, killing, war and poverty. The Creator and Gia have answered our prayers. We as a group are restoring heaven on earth. The Garden of Eden will be in bloom again. We will have the ability to manifest all that we want into existence almost instantly. We will be able to live extremely long lives while staying young, depending on how well we treat our avatars. We will be able to leave anytime we want as our three-dimensional version of Earth has been quarantined to keep the darkness in. The souls that don't ascend will have a time where their reality will get worse and worse. This has already started. There will be food shortages, killing, the things they talk about in the end times in the Freemason King James version of the Bible. If the evil ones don't turn their hearts towards love and compassion for all living beings, respecting and honoring all beings and each other then they will be recycled. At this time those that held on to fear and hate in their hearts will be judged by the creator. If she deems this being to not be worthy to hold love in its heart then it will be sent to the central sun and terminated. Which means for the first time they will truly die and cease to exist as a singular entity. What's meant when we say recycle is to earth die. We are eternal and most have died on earth many times. Our physical existence is the fleeting dream, it's our existence on the other side as a light being that's the real us.

Chapter 11

The New Earth

This tale is a story of two worlds. A tale of light and dark. A split in the reality that the collective experiences. We as individuals can now access higher dimensions by raising our vibrations and aligning our thoughts to the truth. This is the tale people call the new earth, which is kind of funny because it's always been there. It was just not accessible to the collective. It was blocked off by the dark forces that are in play. This was accomplished by building a prison of certain beliefs. The darkness thinks it's going to hijack themselves into the next incarnation of earth. They have successfully achieved this before, four times before. Reptilians have the ability to time travel, in sessions they explain time is like a rubber band. They bend it over like a infinity symbol and where it touches the being can walk between time. This is not going to be allowed this time. It has already been arranged by the light beings here. The only beings that don't know this are the dark ones. The Creator is seeing to this personally. She has asked me to write a book telling of her story where she came here herself to oversee this so it wouldn't be messed up again. There won't be a fifth time. Period. Clint how do you know this information? I had a session with a very attractive woman. Her eyes were the most magical I'd ever seen, with ISIS a strong second. So, in Quantum healing we ask for the client to give us questions to ask their higher self. Her list had one question on it. What number in the creation of all beings was she? As I started, I thought this will be crazy. The answer she got was zero. This aspect of the Creator said She is here to fix her mistake. In the past She had left this responsibility to

39

other beings. The reptilians and Freemason were able to jump across the resets in the past. She stated she would handle this personally and that this date would not be let out. It's funny to me that a lot of past life practitioners are dark workers searching the theta realm trying to get a hold of this knowledge. Good luck with that... Creator said that when she meets a person, she instantly judges them on their soul's development, worthy or not worthy. When you look another being in the eyes you never really know who the being is behind those eyes.

By roughly 2025 this split will become permanent. Remember no one will know this date. This event or the rapture as the Christians know it as will happen in the middle of the night. People will wake up and some people will be gone. The face of the earth will be changed in a single night. Have you seen the daily earth quakes? That time is for sure near. The souls that go to the new earth vibration will experience a new world filled with oneness. They will rebuild the earth from all the damage that has been done by terraforming, wars, killing and negativity; all orchestrated by the darkness. The darkness brought this on themselves. They tried and succeeded in taking over the earth for a time. Greed will bring the dark to their ruin. Those that harbor duality and negativity and those refusing to turn from the dark ways will experience death for the first time ever! These souls will be recycled to the Great Central Sun. Their energy will be re-purposed to other things. We are now in the time of the tribulations talked about in the Christian Bible. Me personally, I cannot wait to reach the new earth. As I do now experience large glimmers of the higher vibrational energy and it's a beautiful experience!!! You can tell when you're in a high vibrational reality when you look around and the colors are really bright and the general vibration is high.

What an amazing time to be alive. I thank the Creator for allowing me to be the one to bring this message. There are so many amazing souls here and I got to be the one??? Praise to the Most High. One Light, One Love

Chapter 12

Heal Thy Self

The word healthy is a mash up of the words heal and thy. What's the easiest way to combat the epidemic of disease and sickness? Don't get sick. It really is that simple, but there are blocks to bringing this into reality. The people that are sick, see other people and tell them they have a disease or illness. The mind of the person hearing this then starts creating the illness or disease, all fueled by fear. What people think is the medical caduceus is in fact the staff of Hermes, which represents trade. In this case it is the trade of people. They are farmers of humans just like cattle. They show it off right in front of the general public's eye and you have no clue.

With Quantum hypnosis we are accessing the theta realm. This is the same realm that any magical practitioner accesses or any one that meditates. Now the dark powers that be are programming the collective through the Alpha/ Beta state of hypnosis, which is done by watching television. By viewing TV, humans enter a very light stage of trance. The dark use this as their avenue since for most it's not noticeable. Throw your TV out or only use it for research and occasional movies. And whatever you do… DO NOT WATCH THE NEWS!!!

To understand what and how Quantum healing and past life regression work, one must understand what the energies are. Next, how to correlate them to the human in the avatar. The subconscious or over soul also known as the Higher Self. In terms of percentage, most of the persons soul is on the other side of the veil. What is the veil? To understand the veil,

41

you must first understand what the earth truly is. The earth as we know it has been greatly miss represented. The earth is all energy, it's an energy ball as seen from the outside. This is easily proven with any $40.00 telescope. Just look up at a star and what do you see? An energy ball that is moving and spinning. This is why they tell people that the earth is spinning and people believe it. At the soul level we know this to be a truth. But once in the earth energy, we are inside that spinning energy. The earth we live on is not and does not spin. The Earth is flat and the North Pole is at the center and the South Pole points to the outside of the circle. If you want more evidence search operation High Jump with Freemason Admiral Bird. This is where they were trying to see if they could get out from the edge of the firmament. Then research Operation Fishbowl in 1962, nuclear missiles were shot up against the firmament. This ignorant action could have wiped out all of the life on here on earth. They were not thinking about all of creation here, only about their own selfish motives.

Humans are a funny species. Put an animal in a cage and they will repeatedly check to make sure they are still trapped but go about their daily life. You put a human in a cage and the human will ask why? They couldn't have people asking why am I in an extremely big cage? NASA, the fake space program was invented just shortly after this to convince people that humans could leave this realm in the current physical form. The truth is that no person has ever left this earth realm in human form.

Chapter 13

The Colonization of Earth

The reptilians took over with an asteroid attack here on earth. Taking control of the earth back from The Pleiades, whom had created humans as a slave race. This lowered the collective consciousness dramatically. Killing most of the inhabitants. This was allowed by the powers that be so as to fast track the evolution of humanity. The darkness engineered these denser bodies that we know inhabit and created a slave race of humans. The tale of this is in the Sumerian tablets. The race that created the new humans were Pleiadian, and had six fingers. This is the reason why American Indians would show their hands with only five fingers, to say I am one of the good beings.

The American Indians were given a very specific task. They are the protectors of the earth. I personally find it rather funny that after 400 years of extermination it was the American Indians that was the catalyst to bring down the empire. After the last cataclysm which was by fire, the Magi of Egypt brought American Indians to Egypt, took them underground and sparred them from total destruction . This is why the cave art we see depicts the Ant people. This is a reference to the people that lived under the mounds, or pyramids. they are to carry a message and to watch for the signs. These signs are the Blue Star Kachina Prophecy of the Hopi. The ancient prophecy states that when the Blue Star Kachina appears in the heavens, the Fifth World will emerge. The Hopi name for the star Sirius is Blue Star Kachina. Then there is the Black Snake Prophecy. The Black snake prophecy is the signal announcing the second coming of Christ conscientiousness or as the Indians know it as the Rainbow Wave. The Rainbow Wave will unite the four races of man. How ironic the race of people that was almost wiped out by the Christians is the race that saved the earth and ushered in the Christ consciousness. The Indians are true Christians as we all were before the Catholic church re framed the world as we know it today.

This time is here now, bringing love to the world for all that will turn away from their wicked ways. Such things killing, murder, greed and plundering of the planet. Humanity is evolving from duality into Oneness. The darkness will not be making this evolution. This time of duality is ending. It served its purpose and is no longer needed. The real problem here is that the darkness tried to take over everything, and nearly succeeded.

The darkness did everything they could to deter this awakening. They created war and killed over 60 million beings. They orchestrated 911 attack. Then they made laws to restrict them like forced inoculations. Then purposely gave the Indians small pox, these people suffered horribly under American occupation with untold horrors. But so great is the spirit of the American Indian, they remembered the truth then handed down the oral tradition.

The American Indians were on time and anyone that is going to enjoy the new earth owes them a debt of gratitude for being strong and connected. I personally offer free sessions to any indigenous Americans. It's time to start healing the wounds the United States government, the fake Christians and the darkness has inflicted upon these very important beautiful people.

The Indians were given a magical staff from the Magi of Egypt. The white magicians were mighty in their power. They were told to stick it in the ground every night and the way it pointed in the morning was the direction they would travel the next day. It was their compass to ensure they travel to the correct destination.

They moved about for years then one day they stopped for the night. When they stuck the staff into the ground that night a horrible storm ensued. When they awoke in the morning, they saw that the staff was not disturbed. The staff was still strait up, perfectly vertical. This was the sign they had been waiting for. They had arrived at the location they would inhabit until the time of the Rainbow Wave.

This directly relates to the tale of two earths. Today we call this the new earth but in reality, it has always been here. Where do you think the Mayans went? During a past ascension approximately 800 earth years ago they ascended. This is why the Mayan ruins still look so new because they are not that old. The Mayans came together and ascended the majority of their civilization as a group. The ones that were left were the ones you hear about performing sacrifices and the other unspeakable acts. When you sacrifice a human and say the rites associated with that act, it enables darker beings to enter our reality in the physical form. They are not supposed to be here and are interloping in this vibration. It also allows the person to be able to stay young and cheat death. As well as many other dark things that can be done with ritual sacrifice blood magic.

Chapter 14

The New World Order

One should ask? what was the old-world order? The old-world order was Tartary (Latin: Tartaria Magna), the great Tartary at its height was a worldwide peaceful culture.

The Catholic Reformation of 1781, was the darkness reforming the earth realm to reduce the collective consciousness into a lower vibration. That put humans into survival mode. They did this through killing and poverty. Before this event, which was timed with the last grand solar minimum, people were struggling to stay warm and feed themselves. The catholic church took advantage of this and used biological warfare as well as religious doctrine to reform the planet as we know it now. These Freemasons and Jesuits are known by their hiding of their hands in photos, it's called the hidden hand signal, think Napoleon, Ted Cruz etc. A quick google search will reveal many of these dark beings that have covered up our true history. Also do a google search on the masonic M hand sign.

The last remaining people that lived the old way were pitted against each other and made to fight wars. This was done through the use of dark magic and media indoctrination as well as the use of conjuring spirits to attach to those that wouldn't subject to their rule. After a spirit has been conjured and given orders to manipulate a human it has no choice but to complete its task. The most powerful force on earth is a human being in a body, besides the divine will of the Creator or Gia it's the human being that is next. These Freemasons trap these souls into the brass vessel..so named to hide the fact that its iron, Iron cannot be crossed by negative entities and a vessel with one trapped inside would be a prison for that enslaved being.

As this book hits print, many will speak out about it in anger. A human reaction after being brain washed to truth is anger. This anger comes from the fact that the person that's been indoctrinated hears information that conflicts their created version of reality. This response will be the proof that the truth is out. There is no turning back now. As we used to say in special operations. It's GO time!

Chapter 15

Ascending

As I began practicing past life regression and Quantum healing, all this massive knowledge about what's going on here on earth began coming forward. Trust me the darkness is using these techniques as well as the light to change the collective consciousness. Also, to gain and disseminate information. The biggest thing the darkness is looking for would be the date of the coming reset. This information is what has enabled them to jump into the next evolution before.

The darkness is using the quantum realm to program the many beings that are in play here. During a quantum session the word "they", is used in reference to the higher selves' guides, guardians, the angelic realm, the light councils and the Creator herself. They started sending me clients with information about what's coming and cannot be stopped. It is for the highest good of all and was asked for by us, the collective consciousness. There will be a choice made by each human to support and stay in the collective 3rd dimensional reality, or to make the ascension. The 3rd dimensional reality will be basically the end of times described in the Bible. There will be horrible things going on such as severe weather causing food shortages, mass sickness, fighting over resources and death. This is to facilitate learning for those souls that are younger and have not learned all the necessary lessons yet. There will be a specific time period given to these souls to learn. If they do not turn to the light by the end, they will die for the first time ever and be recycled to the central sun. Their energy will be used to create new energy, planets, rocks and more.

I was sent a client on June 1, 2018. During this session I was told several things. First was that the rift in the astral was created by us using blood magic and sacrifice. The portal was then sealed by the light Magi of this planet, the Arch Angels and all the light forces or ETs that are here for this fight. I personally participated in this fight but being a young magician, I felt that I didn't have the skills for combat so I rose to the astral plane and supported their efforts by channeling energy to the forces of light. I was told that any dark energy left on Earth was for training for the younger souls so they could learn their lessons. The old karma system was now turned off and a new super karma was in effect. This new Karma is super-fast and is twofold. It helps those on the right track by controlling their thoughts and emotions in a positive way. In a state of oneness, they will put love first and have the ability to manifest the new world. This new, faster karma will allow those that cannot control their thoughts of negativity and anger to manifest those things into reality. This is to teach them to change their ways. It's a learning tool that will help them save themselves. Karma is very, very real.

I was also told that the Light had already secured victory and that the darkness cannot defeat or hijack its way into the next evolution. The dark has been able to that the last four times we have tried to rid the planet of that darkness. This time it has been guaranteed by the Creator that the light will overcome the darkness. Also, the darkness will be handled personally by Spirit, that way no errors can be made. We are to focus on creating the new world. As I write this book the worlds are simultaneously existing. There is evidence of this all around us, The Mandela effect, news articles of food shortages, riots and all kinds of crazy things happening. On the other hand, you do hear and see evidence of great new technology coming out as well. People are moving off the grid, taking their kids back from the system, creating places for retreats and communal living. Humans are evolving, some of us can move between the worlds as we are multidimensional, all could if they develop their skills.

But there are few that can be multidimensional at this present time. This is funny to me because there are so many using past life regression trying to find out when the event will occur. They will not be given this information. There are many dark workers using this truth that an event is coming, to spread fear about it. This is dangerous because that fear is what the darkness uses against the people. After this event 60 percent of the population will be gone. By gone I mean the two vibrational realities will be separated, And the ones left will come together to create the new world. A world that is all about love and oneness as we are all truly all one, we will collaborate and support each other. We will be sharing everything we have. There will be a time with no money but there will be a barter system installed shortly after. We just won't care about money the way we do now. There will be no charging for camping any place on earth or for food or utilities. We will develop free energy to support our new earth. We can live as long as we want to. The human body is made to heal itself. The firmament will cease to exist in its present form as well as free will. These abilities will not be instantly attainable as change takes time. We can leave whenever we'd like to go. We will have the ability to stay a couple hundred years then switch out with another soul that wants to come in. People say why would you want to live that long? We will be able to stop the aging process at any age and stay there for as long as we would like. Now that would that be fun! Getting to see all the beautiful things on this planet... I personally cannot wait.

All anyone has to do is sit down and meditate and set the intention that they want to go to the new earth. Then ask for guidance and turn away from the slave system. Start learning how to be self-supportive and self-sufficient. Their higher self will guide them on the path, which will usually include a Quantum healer. No one goes to the new earth with any past life Karma, no one. This is the hidden message that the being we know as Jesus Christ came to teach us. Christ was here to show us how to get off the karmic hamster wheel.

The time of the split is fast approaching and we should all prepare to the best of our ability. Learning how to grow your own food, provide for your own being and to live in harmony with all beings. This is an evolution that we won't start out with everything given to us. We must learn and come together to achieve harmony. We created new earth and we will build the new world together. With our new manifesting capabilities, we will rapidly grow the new world.

There will be retreats set up to bring those to that are asking to leave the 3rd dimensional slave system. Once they have had enough slavery, killing and suffering. There are those of us that will guide them to these retreats. Once there they will receive healing and reeducation. There will be much to learn about the way this new realm works and how to control thoughts and emotions to live in oneness peacefully.

These healing centers are going up now in places around the world. It's truly a beautiful thing to see this new world emerge. I thank the Creator for allowing me to have lived at this time. In the future all generations will talk about what has happened during this time. The 144,000 are ushering in a new evolution of humanity. What a beautiful time to be alive.

Chapter 16

Lessons

This life I have chosen has been an extremely difficult life to live. I never fit in with any group. I have always been singled out and picked on for being different and not thinking the same way as most. I have always been a very sensitive person. Add to that the fact that I chose to bring this message forward for all to hear and to expose the truth will require my full attention. I have been attacked personally and through magic from Freemasons and dark beings on all levels. Also, by indoctrinated younger souls who are taught to lash out at those that are different. As the warriors of light awaken from their slumber, the darkness has been able to see our light our whole lives. Relate this to standing in a room in the pitch dark and your holding a flashlight. Everyone can see you but you cannot see the others around you. This is what it's like to have been a lightworker in this time of the awakening. It's not been an easy road. I have seen many lightworkers quit and commit suicide as this road we travel is not an easy journey. Many are choosing to help from the other side of the veil, this is why so many people are dying right now. Many have been lost to traps the darkness has set up the drugs and control systems like fake truther sites, such as Alex Jones. But mostly the fear is whats used to control humans here.

The truth be told, we actually failed and that allowed the forces of light to regroup and rewind time to ensure that victory would be guaranteed. This is why there is so much Mandela effect, Deja Vue and forgetfulness plaguing society at the present time. This is a side effect of having to rewind this time line we are presently living within. The forces of light are victorious. The light will always overcome the darkness.

However, all important positions are held and controlled by the Freemasons. You cannot work in the system and get a fair shake unless you be quiet and a good debt slave. The only way to succeed and move on towards the new earth vibration is to walk away from the control system as much as possible. At the present one cannot completely walk away from their current life however; each day brings new technology and opportunities that allow us to turn away from the current system. People are doing this more and more. Eventually it will reach all whom are able to learn and grow into beings ready for the new earth.

I personally chose to live a different way. I live a more nomadic lifestyle. As I learn I will be able to guide others in this process. This has been a lonely road to travel as there are not many people doing this at the present. But each day the movement grows as more and more people are tired of slaving their lives away and getting nowhere.

It's crazy when I travel into lower vibrational realities and people talk about how horrible the world is, I laugh because in my world I don't see those things. Almost all these people live in a world where they watch the news. There is a reason it's called programming, its hypnotizing people into the Alpha/Beta state of trance. To escape the 3rd dimensional reality you must control what information is force fed into your mind. Guard your mind as your subconscious sees everything. If something or someone is negative, separate yourself from them. We are here to save no one. As we save ourselves it will raise our vibration and allow us to carry more light. That light will activate more people to this awakening. Just being alive and carrying that light will allow the awakening to be a success. During the last ascension, the dark used religious indoctrination to convince people that there was severe weather and food shortages because people were using magic. So, they dragged people out of their homes and burned them or worse. These were the imprisoned lightworkers that were here to carrying the light. This is why we hear of the witch trials and the inquisition. Each human carries a light inside them. The lightworkers carry a lot more light than younger souls. This is why the dark had to kill the witches and warlocks in the name of their god. Because as long as they are alive, they anchor the light into the earth realm. But we all came here with a specific plan to be carried out in this lifetime. If you do not know what your life path is, I suggest you find a Quantum healer. Once you get a past life regression done this will assist your awaking and reveal your contractual path. Now, I must make it very clear that every single decision you make will change your timeline. I have seen some of my clients make good decisions for their highest and best such as service to others, they literally jump timelines to a higher vibrational reality. This can also be done by practicing a manifesting technique called Quantum time jumping. This is done by going to sleep visualizing that you already live in a higher vibrational reality.

To accomplish my mission, I have lost my family of almost ten years including a son I adopted, all my possessions and 99 percent of my friends. Everyone called me crazy and other not so nice words. The path of service to a higher calling has not been easy. Most of our soul family that is here to support each other is very spread out at the present. I could not have ever accomplished my mission without them. Thank you all and you know who you all are. I love each and every one of you. But there will be a time soon when we will come together. This information is starting to come out in my client's sessions now. The truth is emerging.

Chapter 17

Graduation

I would like to speak now about what to expect as a general overview when a soul starts to make the transition into the new earth energies. I am calling this graduation. To graduate there will be tests right? This is no different.

Some point each lightworker that is making the transition will have to make the choice to start walking away from the things that are bad for them. If they don't listen to their guidance things can go terribly wrong. I didn't listen to my higher self and I tried to take my family with me. This ended up going horribly wrong since my wife, at the time, had chosen to experience a different reality. The funny thing was that she was actually very awake and on her path. But she made one very bad decision which was to start sleeping to her ex while we were still married. In her defense we were both attacked by a Freemason Roger Binnit from my work. It struck me strange why he would be outside my house taking a picture of it? I removed the one we found attached to me. It showed me the magic that conjured it then you could see the checkerboard floor as it left on its mission from the freemason lodge where they practice their magic ,to came attach to me and manipulate my life. It changed her entire life path. So, when we don't follow our guidance there are serious repercussions. I knew my higher self was telling me to separate from my wife but I didn't listen. The result was our break up was awful and quite hurtful.

I personally failed many tests, but there were many opportunities to try again and again. Then after several tries, I was able to operate with a loving intention, as much as I could. Then my life started to evolve to the new earth energies. To other lightworkers living in the system thinking one day a new life will magically appear, that's not the way it works. It is all our perception. You manifest your reality. This is an individual test. You as a creator must create this life, I have noticed that people's higher selves are guiding them to me to show them how to live and to be able to ascend as I have already started the process myself. The biggest advice I can give anyone going through graduation is to make every decision out of love for yourself first and the highest love of others next. There are those that will disagree and that's ok. I am speaking about what I have seen work best for others as they go through this process.

I recommend people start meditation daily and have a Cosmic Quantum Awakening clearing and healing session and then also a past life regression. The clearing and healing session will remove any and all negative energies that have collected during this life. Also, we can heal any and all illnesses and diseases by using this method. The past life regression will release any past life karma and show the client their life path. This process will jump start their path by an estimated ten years. During the clearing and healing session, I also go over every chakra. This is to ensure the energetic body is functioning properly and at its highest and best. I also open the two new chakras. We have access to a chakra that is above the crown chakra called the soul star chakra. This is only given to star seeds. The other is open to all souls that are going to the new earth and they call this the new earth Sephra. This chakra enables us to ground to and use the new earth energies, I have clients that are on an ascension path that is not taking them to the new earth. They don't have the earth chakra opened up yet. The higher self will be the guide to whether or not it's able to be opened during a session.

There are many different beings here, some are all love, some are warriors here for the fight and some are transmuters that naturally transmute negative energies into positive energies, almost unknowingly to the conscious mind. This is difficult concept for most to understand that the All is love for all beings. To understand this, you have to expand your consciousness to see a bigger picture. Speak your truth but remember all truths are but half-truths. This is according to the perspective of the viewer. You see what you wish to see.

Chapter 18

The Coming Deception

A fake alien invasion is a big trump card the Dark has planned and its being fueled by many aspects. The movies show the earth being invaded by aliens and we have to fight them to survive. Ronald Freemason Reagan said it best, "if only there was an outside force to make the people come together as one?" What he didn't say next was it would be easy to control them then.

Before this "invasion" happens, they will claim the fake space station was destroyed by an asteroid. The alien invasion will then play out. The ruling cabal has very advanced technology kept hidden such as anti-gravity machines, weapons technology and more. These things will be used to deceive people. The Dark is also using past life regression sessions that are fake. They want to tell false stories about aliens and wars. You need to know that any session that preaches fear is not of the light. There is no galactic war. The funniest thing to me is this galactic federation of light. The beings that are here are from many different galaxies. Why would they use the word galactic? There are millions of multiverses out there. Secondly, why would they call themselves an earth name like federation? People don't always use discernment. The game we play while we are here is one between the light and the dark. The real hidden secret is that there are a lot of beings here from different planets, realms, dimensions. These are just different vibrational realities. Each planet teaches a certain subject. Earth school is for learning how to manage your emotions. I am cataloging my findings now for a later book. The extra-terrestrials are us, the humans. Not all humans are ET's but some are. I personally started my individual soul incarnation in the Pleiades on a Terra (with ground) planet. There are water Pleiadean planets as well. I was what is called in earth language, a quantum mechanic, which means I worked with the energies needed to establish new planets. I helped set up earth and get it ready for life. To do this we use two or three suns depending on the amount of light and heat needed. Earth needed two suns to set up then after the desired conditions were reached, we turned off one sun. This is called the dark sun or the Saturday sun. It also explains why we can mysteriously predict the eclipses. They magically appear to be the same size. They are all the same size. The sun, the moon and the dark sun are all approximately 500 miles high and 30 miles wide. This is easy to calculate by tracing the sun's rays through the clouds and using math to calculate the angles. Math never lies. Math is the language of creation and of the Creator. This is how I came to understand the forces at play here on earth. There are so many energies on earth. We have come to learn to control those energies. This is why I was guided to quantum healing, why it comes naturally to me and why I am able to teach it to others.

Another great deception is the false truth that people are trapped here. We volunteered to come to earth to help. The only beings trapped here in the physical, are the darkness and the reptilians. They truly are trapped here and will never be allowed to leave. All they think about is how to get out of their prison. It's their own fault as they were never meant to be here. They also should not have enslaved the whole planet.

All the earths governments are controlled by different factions of extra-terrestrials. Some light and some dark ETs. The United States of America is one of the darkest as well as England the Vatican and the Catholic church. Russia is actually of the light. Speaking of Russia and the holy land that's mentioned in the bible, Jerusalem is actually the

Kremlin. The work of A.T. Fomenko, G.V. Nosovsky clearly proves this. The land in Israel or ISIS Ra and EL was purchased during World War I. 33rd degree Freemason Winston Churchill made the deal to get the land in Palestine then 33rd degree Freemason Harry Truman was the major player in creating the state of Israel. This was to be used to create World War III. However, this war will be the war of Armageddon. Freemason and southern General Albert Pike spoke about this in letter dated August 15, 1871. Oddly this is exactly the spot where world peace will start. People of different faiths will put down their arms and they will not fight any longer.

As I work with past life regressions, I am seeing an agenda coming through a lot of sessions. First let's talk about the accuracy of what these people are publishing as facts. I noticed early on that if a person had attachments of a darker nature, the entity could manipulate the information that was seen and conveyed by the clients. All of which I documented and passed on to the other practitioners. Now lets take a look at the dynamic we have going, We were given this past life regression but not told that entities not in human form could manipulate these sessions. The darkness which uses these out of body beings now has a avenue to effect thousands of people. A glass full of water has no room for more water. These practitioners didn't want to look at the research and they definitely didn't want to hear another point of view about what was going on. Any past life regression where the client is not cleared of attachments and negative thought forms are non-valid. That is because there is no way to determine if the information has been altered by any dark beings dwelling within their vessel. This convoluted information is being used to program people that hear it to believe there is a galactic war. When we communicate with beings that we cannot see its important to know who and what we are talking to, Any past life regression that the client has not been cleared is convoluted.

It is very suspicions that dark forces never get named. Normally they are referred to as "they" or "dark". The dark beings convoluting the information won't name those in control. After the many years of the light struggling with dark, both sides know all the players yet the "galactic federation of light" won't name who they are up against either. This all seems very odd to me. I personally do not trust any information that comes from a client that's not been cleared.

Chapter 19

The Unknown

As soon as I started on this journey a lot of strange things started happening. I was visited by a being that was clearly a reptilian. They are easy to spot for an empath. First you feel the vibrational control they can assert over a human, it's almost like mind control. The first thing that was weird about this client was that I instantly had an attraction to her. The second was during her session she self-healed as soon as I said this must happen. The next thing that stuck out was how young she looked. I'm seeing this in all the reptilians that I come across. They are able to control their age through vibration. Reptilians are masters at vibration. Queen Elizabeth must be thousands of years old. The next thing happened after her session. She had so much control over me, I would have got on the ground and licked her feet if she asked me. At this point I realize I was being controlled and I used mentalism to overcome this. I set an intention, I stated that my human eyes would see what I was actually looking at in my mind's eye. This is when things got really weird. I was looking at her face her eyes started changing. It was like she was phasing in and out of reality. I see why they call these beings shape shifters. As she was leaving, she said, "you should fix things with your wife". At this point I didn't know there was any issue with my wife. A short while later it became apparent that was a very big problem with my wife.

Chapter 20

Dr Johny

This Freemason finds me at a meet up group for metaphysical topics and instantly wants to be my best buddy. We do a couple of sessions and he wants to work with me. After talking a while, he tells me he worked for the CIA, when he joined, they told him welcome to the Fourth Reich. He says Nazis run the United States. Then he tells me that he's a Jesuit priest and that he's a doctor. Riding in his car there is a masonic police badge that he carries. Time after time he brags about killing people, having sex and the only important thing is making money. He says he would have no problem killing more people if they get in his way. I decide to cut off all contact with him. A couple months later he shows up again and this time I notice he's using magic to collect information from me. Research the Seals of Solomon and you will see that these are magical talismans attributed to the biblical King Solomon. The seals are said to be powerful and have the ability to control others, especially when charged with planetary magic. There are many Freemason lodges, if one human is powerful, imagine what a group can create as a collective consciousness?

Fast forward to one of the days I was writing this book, the doctor calls me and starts asking who my business partners are? He wants to work with me and he knows the prime minister of the Philippines. He apparently got this information from Facebook. He wanted to know where I was at presently. He has obviously been trying to follow me and my work. Why, one would ask. Why would this guy be so persistently trying to contact me?

The next weird client I had was an older woman in her mid-70s but looked about 40. Instantly I'm suspicious. We do a clearing and healing session and she has no attachments which is either a sign of a reptilian or a very advanced being. Only the true humans seem to have the attachments, she did have some thought forms, we transmuted those into positive energies to help her on her path. I heal the light and the dark.

During the session she says she is a diplomat for the federation of light and she was a federation police officer. Before that and she had hunted reptilians and that once she had found a lair. In that lair she saw dead humans in the process of being eaten. Also, she saw that the female eggs are purple. Is this why the world's public leaders wear purple ties? A very wise person once said that the world is run by signs, symbols and colors. During the session she was telling me how they can manipulate time and time travel, which is absolutely possible as all time exists now. After the session I tried to call her a couple of times to touch base. I talk to my clients after their sessions to make sure they got the email and remind them to download the session to keep it to re-watch for continued healing. Maybe 1% of the time a person can have an entity able to hide from the body scan. Afterward that darkness can retaliate against the client, give them physical pain and anxiety type issues. After repeatedly trying both calls and texts to reach the woman, about a week later she texts me and tells me she is busy in meetings. Fast forward to her next session, I recommend all people do two sessions. One a clearing and healing session to get their physical health in top shape and to get the energetic body performing correctly. Then about five days later a past life regression session, this gives the client their life path and removes any past life karma they might be carrying. There is absolutely no way to tell if a person is carrying past life karma unless you do a session. The day of her past life regression, about an hour before the session, she starts texting to ask where her recording is? I tell her she was supposed to download it. She flips put and starts getting very aggressive. I log on to a video with her so I can explain it is no problem. I can recover the session but she's furious by this point. She is saying I didn't text her that information. I explain that I tried to call multiple times. At this point she screaming, cussing and throwing things all around the room. I disconnect the video. For hours after she is sending me e-mails threatening me. About a week later she went on the quantum practitioner's forum leaving comments trying to defame my character. The lesson learned here was as an empath my heart told me to not have any more contact with her. I got a bad vibe, which I didn't listen to and it was clearly telling me she was up to no good. The darkness attacks the light. in every way possible. By nature, this is the result with two opposite polarities.

The next client I had was a psychic and I could tell she had a dark nature. I took a vow to help the light and the dark so I had to try to help her too. During her first session she had all kinds of attachments so we cleared them out. The very next day I called her and she tells me that she was up all night in horrible pain. I tell her that we need to do another session immediately. We find more attachments which I also removed. The next day she was upset saying the entity had done all the talking. I explain that is not possible, especially when the entity is not attached to the head or crown Chakra. Her attachments had been in her belly, this is why she had pain in her stomach. A week went by and we start to do her past life regression. She tells me that I must ask all her questions in order. I never ask the questions in the order given to me. I find more accurate answers come if I skip around. I start to ask her questions and I get out of order and I could tell her higher self was getting upset. Then I asked her higher self if the entity we had just removed did all the talking during her last session? The next I feel is her energy attacking me. I didn't even know this was possible. It hurt extremely badly, causing so much physical pain I had to call my lightworker soul family to send healing. That healing was the only way for me to get passed the pain and move on.

Clinton Withrow Jr.

The next day she was on the quantum healing forum bad mouthing me. She had omitted the fact that she had energy attacked me during the session. Once again, the darkness attacks any way it can.

The odd thing is that during her session she said that smoking cigarettes, killing and eating animals is all okay. She also talked about after leaving earth they will travel in space ships to find another planet to inhabit. At the time I didn't realize that the darker beings use space ships and travel the cosmos. The light beings use portals and just step from one planet to another as they are multidimensional. The darkness is not truly multidimensional so they need a spaceship to protect them. Anyone with any discernment can listen to the recordings and tell she's a darker being.

My next strange visit was from a girl that found me on a dating site. I could tell she was a very powerful being. She was an extremely sexy woman with very small frame. She said she was a doctor that had been a bank robber before becoming a doctor, she also was a pharmacist. I could tell she had the ability to control reality. I would have a thought and she would look at me, she could read my thoughts. We did a session and I found no attachments. She had the ability to self-heal as she once had cancer and had cured herself by raising her vessels vibrations, this is the cure for cancer as a high vibration doesn't let and disease grow.. Her session was cut short by due to circumstances beyond my control.

After the session she told me she came to save me and to heal my heart which struck me as odd. As our relationship progressed, I could tell when I would have a thought, she could read my mind. A few days later we were intimate and she made sounds like purring, not like a cat purring but more like a reptile. She like to be violent and rough during sex. I started to realize she had sought me out to find out what I knew and what I was doing. I let her read the first draft of my book. She tried to convince me I was wrong. But I wouldn't budge about not publishing this book. Within hours she decided we were done. She vanished as quick as she

68

entered. After much meditation I was told she was a reptilian Freemason. She would talk with her hands using Freemason hand signs. And who would hire a convicted felon doctor? Unless you have connections that's just not going to happen. I hold onto the fact that there are good reptilians as well as bad. I could be wrong, time will tell.

Some of the first information that came through my earlier sessions was that the darkness is made up of all kinds of beings, not just reptilians. The reptilians are the human's sister race from Mars. One version got empathy and the other got the ability to master vibration and no empathy. One could ask with no empathy how could they be good hearted beings? I guess only time will tell the answer to that question.

I have heard many negative comments when I tell people my story. The bottom line is this, I came here to experience all that this world has to offer. I personally do believe there are good beings in all races. I hope this to be true. This time of the rainbow wave is for us all to come together, light and dark, the beings from different realms and planets. I am trying to be the change that's needed, not only here but from all around the multiverse.

Two days after breaking up with the Freemason reptilian doctor, a crazy thing that happened to my RV in the middle of the night. I heard a very loud bang and found the awning ripped off the trailer. I thought it was wind damage but after the sun came up, I saw my solar panel (weighing about 25 pounds) on top of the RV and it was not moved. Clearly the wind was not the cause. I found the aluminum pipe that was snapped in half. It was extremely strong, so strong I could not dent it with a hammer. I estimate that it took at least 1500 pounds of force to break that pipe.

In meditation I was told that there was an attack in the astral and that it was repelled by the forces of light, or angels. As above so below, if something happens in the astral then there will be signs here and vice versa. This was definitely a head scratchier. Spirit told me to move that day to a new, unknown location. There are many things about this world that we have no knowledge of yet.

Chapter 21

The Grand Finale

We all know this whole thing is building up to a grand finale. This will be a split in the realities, the Rapture. Every good being is in on the operation. Even the Creator herself is here to handle the change over. We have attempted this split four times before but it was unsuccessful. The information got out and the darkness was able to hijack themselves into the next evolution. The tales of great cataclysms was the light trying to rid itself from the darkness. Like a bad case of fleas, we were not successful until this time. This time we got it right. The light timed the ascension with the correct planetary alignments. This includes the individual planetary alignments to support the lightworkers with their specific tasks. We as the human civilization will not be doing a reset like cataclysmic events have done in the past. This ascension is about creating another evolution. Moving into a Christ centered world.

The darkness will not be making this evolution. As the earth's vibration raises, the reptilian controllers will not be able to stay cloaked anymore. They will have to leave or be hunted to extinction. They operate as a collective or as a hive mind and they will choose to leave together. I recently talked to a Freemason and he had told me that he was leaving the country soon. He urged me to join him. I believe here in the U.S. things are going to get very real, very soon. It is graduation time. Let the show begin. This information will create fear in those that harbor fear. This is the reality of what happens here on earth. Earth is a god school where we come to learn how to control our energy, thoughts and emotions.

There are ways to practice magic that will not cause harm to others. We must practice so that we don't accidentally harm anyone. This is why we are here, to learn to heal and use our divine powers for good. This life on earth is a game with both risks and rewards. Everything here is just a bio mechanical simulation. We feel emotions greatly as part of the learning. We are here for many lessons about love, oneness and to come together for the highest good. We must learn to control our emotions and our thoughts. Our thoughts become our words and thus our reality. Each human generates their own timeline, all the characters in it as well as their reality.

One must understand that as a group we also generate a collective timeline that also influences our group reality. The study of how these timelines work and affect us can become a very deep rabbit hole called string theory. I'm not sure we possess enough intelligence at this particular time to fully understand it all.

The bottom line here is to relax, death is definitely not something to be scared about. Dolores Cannon talks about how dying it is just like getting up from one chair and sitting in another chair. Death should be celebrated, as being in spirit form is our natural state. A true death is very rare meaning you have been sent back to Central Sun. I have had sessions with fallen angels that lost their composure and got emotional and killed thousands in a single moment. They were given additional chances and sent back to god school for reform. Earth is that god school. Creator or the Divine doesn't want your worship. Spirit wants you to find the GOD within you, to connect with your higher self and become part of the collective consciousness, to find your way back home to Source. We are here to learn to help each other as we all are one and we are in this experience together.

Say Hello to the bad guys!

The controlling powers have been aware of this light versus dark battle for thousands of years. You can see illustrated by this masonic tracing board with the white and black floor represents the struggle and game between light and dark. The ladder is the ascension and the symbols represent traps set up to catch to souls on their way up the ladder of ascension and you see that the christian cross is the first obstacle to be overcame. There are many other meanings as well. I want to point out all along, the populace has been getting played like a fiddle. The world is but a stage.

The bottom line is it's all a big game. This will be a hard pill to swallow, No, this is all real I can feel it. No, no it's not. Relax, play the game and have fun. Embrace the challenges

73

that come your way, as you were the one that asked for them! Life is not happening to you. You are creating reality. You chose this and your thoughts are generating your reality.

Chapter 22

The Path Forward

As you read this and decide to make the journey to the new earth vibration, here's what to do;

Meditate every day, do not say I'm tired or I'm too busy or whatever excuse you want to say. Like Nike's slogan, "just do it". The only way to fail at meditation is to not do it at all.

State your intention out loud. The spoken word is the most powerful way to manifest. Hints of this are in the bible. For example, how did God create the world? He spoke it into being. Vibrational frequencies combined with thoughts create our environment. State your name and that you invoke the I Am within you and that it's your will and intent to make the transition to the new earth energy so be it. As above, so below and so it is.

Start listening to your instincts and follow your own inner guidance. find a Cosmic Quantum Awakening practitioner and get a clearing and healing and a past life regression session. If those don't go as you wanted you are welcome to contact me. I've been able to guide people into a state of balance in their mind to achieve the connection to their higher self. Some souls have to work at this but can improve within a short time, depending on the inner work one does.

Eat healthy, most have been lied to about what is healthy. This is what's healthy according to all the higher selves that I have spoken with. Nothing out of a box bag or can, Clearly, we all cannot afford this but do your level best. No land animals at all, they are not here for us to eat. This is actually happening naturally for those that are on their path through the ascension. Eat seafood about once a week. No squid, shark, whales, dolphins or turtles. Stick to fish, lobster, crab etc. You can choose to not eat seafood at all but this is our food source. It has been designed that way meaning we do not get any bad karma from eating fish and shellfish. No milk or cheese. This is my personal vice as I'm a cheese lover, so I just try to moderate it. When it's made in a happy way that is chemical free, we will be able to eat more and it will be healthier for us to consume. Help your neighbors and random people. If you have extra, give it way to those in need. If you harbor the greed then you're not going to make the transition

Exercise but do not over exercise. I like yoga, its stretching, mindfulness and a breathing exercise. You can build up your skill level at your own pace.

You must let go of fear. You will and always have been taken care of by your higher self, trust in that.

There is no past or future, only today. Let go of the past memories and focus on living in this day. Do something fun for yourself every day.

Self-love and self-care are the corner stones to your success in this incarnation.

Drink water distilled water if you can. Bless your water and all food before consuming. This will elevate your vibration.

Water is paramount to our survival. Then there is White powder Ormus, one of the most powerful tools we have. It decalcifies the pineal gland, gives you spiritual energy and connects you with your higher self. This cannot be stressed enough. Ours can be found on ETSY at the Heavenly supplements store. Ormus also known as Mana is paramount to integrating your higher self into your vessel. This is what the ascended masters have done in the past.

Ask any lightworker for help or guidance, as this is why they came here. Their mission to assist others on their journey up the ascension ladder. We all want to live on the new earth in a Christ or Love centered life together as One.

Chapter 23

Why the New Earth?

Why All this fuss about this? Why can't I just work and go home and be happy? The human species in its present form was created to be a slave race. But our geneticist the great ENKI knew one day we would be able to rise above the slavery. And because of this act of defiance the humans have suffered. Suffered for a means to an end. What if Enki was Lucifer? That would put a whole different spin on the once mentioned bad guy of the bible? An end to the slavery. We as humans are on the dawn of ascending the human race to a higher collective level which will mean for the first time ever, we humans will be the masters of our destiny. The Garden of Eden will be open again. In a matter of 50 years the earth will not even look the same as it does now. There will be the reset that changes the earths landscape. Then there will be the Rainbow Warriors that heal and rebuild the earth. Even 5 years from now the earth will not resemble the reality today.

As I raise my vibrations, I start to access the 5th dimensional energies and beyond. The amount of love that felt is massive and is like a drug. The closer we get by being back with the Creator the more love we feel on a daily basis. Let's be real here, love is all anyone of us really wants. This is our ultimate purpose, to find our way back to Source.

Chapter 24

The Way Shower

There are many that have come before us to illuminate the way and to show us the correct path. We call these the Way Showers. I am a Way Shower and I will be greatly criticized for writing this book and speaking out on this subject. But that is what a Way Shower does, lights the way, never minding the potential consequence. They are supported by the Most High and are divinely protected. The Way Showers are supported by all the light beings in the multiverse. The light knows the Way Showers are here to assist the earth and humanity during this time of change. I will travel the world giving lectures and teaching those that are in need. I am teaching Quantum healing now. I am holding sessions for healing and past life regression now. My personal policies are this, I do not charge addicts, suicidal or any terminal illness client. All American Indians get a free session from me.

We live in such a beautiful time. There will soon be an end to disease and illness. We are entering a time of self-supporting communities. A time of love a time of Oneness. A time of freedom. A time that generations after will talk about what we did here together as a group supported by love and powered by Divine will. The Way Showers will shine their light and show us the way, the love and light.

A Note from the Author

This will be one of many short books I write, to convey information. I want to assist during this time of great transition. The next book I write will be on the different star seeds here and different vibrational realities that exist around us. These include all the extra-terrestrials or aliens such as Big Foot or Sasquatch realm, Fae and Faerie realm. The Astral beings that are here. The Atlanteans that are under the water and many more. I will also discuss the Creator being here and why she is here.

All this knowledge is from my work in the Quantum sessions I facilitate. I am not psychic. Psychics talk to beings on the earth plane. Quantum practitioners talk to beings on the other side of the veil or the collective consciousness, the client's higher self, the councils and the Elohim or angelic realm.

I would like to thank the Creator, my Higher self and my team. I know there were times when my team were wondering what is he doing. Sorry about that. I really didn't know there were beings watching everything I was doing. I'd like to say thank you to all the beings of light that are here helping. I'd like to say thank you to all the beings of dark. I believe in you. Go inside yourself and release the fear, seek the light. I'd like to thank my Mom and Dad, Crystal, Anthony, Tricia, all my friends and my soul family. And if you feel I missed you, this thank you is for you. Thank you.

Also, a special thanks to my editor Patricia Walker, you have single handedly restored my faith in humanity.

You came into my life out of nowhere. Teaching me about strength and giving, showing me all the great qualities that you embody. You are the finest example for the rest of us to look up to. THANK YOU.

The fundamental truth is that even a short fleeting life here has many lessons and many beautiful experiences.

Through the trench's humanity has crawled, we as a collective are evolving into better humans.

All this information comes from the quantum healing sessions and past life regressions which are uploaded up on the Cosmic Quantum Awakening YouTube channel for all to see and judge for themselves.

Godspeed.

Made in the USA
Las Vegas, NV
07 December 2020

12248376R10053